# SLEEPING BEAUTY

## THE COLLECTOR'S
## EDITION

# FOREWORD

"What if ...?"

From the first moment an idea for a Disney film begins to take shape to the time it premieres, those magical words spark amazing creativity as artists, writers, composers and designers seek to create what you see on screen.

As artists create hundreds of drawings, paintings, colour studies and concept sketches, a rich body of artwork grows around the film's creation.

The artistic styling of Sleeping Beauty came from the vision of a single art director, Peter Ellenshaw, who created a world reminiscent of Gothic cathedrals and medieval tapestries. His influence is seen in every detail, including the elegant grace of Princess Aurora herself.

We've enriched the pages of this book with rarely-seen art created during the development of Sleeping Beauty. This evocative art has inspired a unique storytelling approach too. The original film story is told in its entirety, but with enriched storytelling that takes you more deeply into the characters' thoughts and emotions, to make them even more believable and compelling.

As you read and share this book, we hope it deepens your appreciation of Sleeping Beauty and touches your imagination with its own magic.

Once upon a time, in a far away land, lived a king and his fair queen.

Many years they had longed for a child, and finally their wish was granted. A daughter was born, and they called her Aurora after the dawn, for she filled their lives with sunshine.

Although the Queen could have had dozens of nursemaids, she wanted to care for her little daughter herself. She wanted her face to be the first her daughter saw in the morning, and her lips to be the last to touch her child's soft cheeks at night. She didn't even mind waking to comfort Aurora at night.

Those late-night moments were the Queen's favourites. She would wrap Aurora in a pink and blue blanket and carry her to the window to gaze at the stars. Then she would sing the old song that all the mothers and grandmothers in her family before her had sung to their daughters.

*"I promise to give all*
*my heart to thee.*
*To be the best*
*mother I can be.*
*So in your heart,*
*you will know it is true:*
*No princess could be*
*more loved than you."*

When the little princess was a month old the queen and king announced a great holiday throughout the kingdom, so that all of high or low estate might pay homage to the infant princess.

Joyfully the people came, bringing gifts and good wishes. Merchants came with lace and silk and satin for Aurora's gowns. Shoemakers came with tiny jewelled slippers, and toymakers brought dolls with golden curls. Nobles in fur and velvet brought lockets and bracelets of silver and gold. Knights in clanking armour rode beneath waving banners to honour the little princess.

Artists, poets, storytellers and musicians brought paintings, poems and songs. Even the poorest villagers offered baskets of fruit and berries, fresh-baked bread and wreaths of fragrant wild flowers.

"Hail Aurora! Long live the Princess Aurora!" they sang as they came up the winding streets of the village and across the great stone bridge to the castle.

The throne room echoed with laughter and chatter as people crowded in, jostling and craning their necks for a glimpse of the baby princess in her silk-draped cradle.

Suddenly trumpets blared, and a herald's voice rang out. "Their Royal Highnesses, King Hubert and Prince Phillip."

King Stefan and the Queen rose to greet their lifelong friend, King Hubert, and his small son. For many years, King Hubert and King Stefan had dreamed of uniting their kingdoms. Today they would announce that Phillip and Aurora would one day marry.

King Hubert led Prince Phillip to the cradle. "Say hello to your bride to be!" He said.

Prince Phillip studied the baby. She didn't look very interesting. She couldn't run races or throw a ball. And she certainly couldn't play knights and dragons. He wondered what all the fuss was about.

But as he started to turn away, the baby princess lifted her chubby pink hands as if reaching for him. Phillip held out a finger, and she grasped it. Phillip made a silly face at her, and she gurgled.

Maybe she wasn't so boring after all, Phillip decided. When she was old enough, maybe he would teach her to ride horses and fight with a sword. If she didn't turn out to be cry baby or a scaredy cat, she might be fun.

"Well, what do you think of her, Phillip, my boy?" King Hubert exclaimed.

Phillip shrugged. "She'll do, I suppose – for a girl," he answered, and everyone in the throne room laughed.

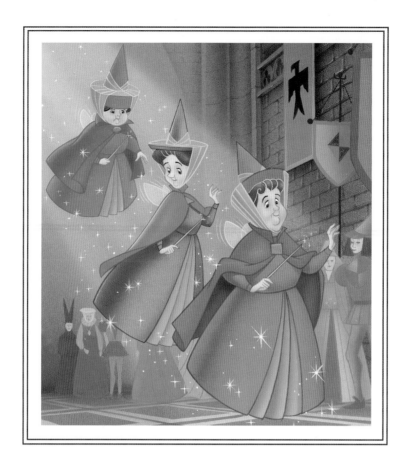

High above the throne room, three sparkling points of coloured light floated in through the windows.

Once again, the herald's voice rang out. "Their most honoured and exalted excellencies, the three good fairies: Mistress Flora, Mistress Fauna and Mistress Merryweather!"

With a sound like the chiming of silver bells, the coloured lights became fairies and drifted down towards the throne.

Flora came forward first. As the oldest of the three fairies by six and one half thousandths of a second, Flora went first in everything. She prided herself on her common sense and ability to tell the others exactly what they should do. She was sure that her gift was the most important. Why, just imagine a princess without my gift, she thought as her feet touched the floor. She was glad she had thought of it first!

She straightened her hat, smoothed her red skirts and bowed to the King and Queen.

Fauna was next to approach the princess. The tender-hearted fairy was very emotional, and a little forgetful. She flitted in circles, trying to remember what her gift to the princess was going to be.

"Oh, dear," she muttered. "What was I going to bestow? Something to do with birds? Wings? Feathers? Oh, no! That can't possibly be right. Who ever heard of a feathered princess?"

As her feet touched the floor, she remembered. Thank heavens, she thought. But I do hope Flora doesn't take too long, or I might forget again. She stood beside Flora, and they both looked up at the third fairy who was flying in large swooping circles around and around above them.

"Why is Merryweather taking so long? She's keeping everyone waiting!" Flora whispered to Fauna.

The fact was, that Merryweather still hadn't decided what to give the Princess. A gift for sewing? Cooking? Gardening, perhaps?

Merryweather pondered as she circled above the thrones. All of those ideas were very practical of course – but not quite right for a princess. What if she gave the Princess the gift of perpetual happiness? No, no, that wouldn't do. What if something sad happened? A princess would look foolish and uncaring if she laughed when something was wrong. Anyway, a person had to feel all the emotions of the heart – not just happiness – in order to grow up as beautiful on the inside as the outside.

"Merryweather, come down here now!" Fauna hissed. "You're embarrassing yourself and us!"

Merryweather sighed. Perhaps she would think of the perfect gift when she saw the baby. As she landed by the cradle, Merryweather jiggled Flora's wings. A sparkling puff of magic dust fell and drifted over the cradle. The baby princess gurgled and tried to catch the sparkles in her fingers.

"Ah! The little darling!" Merryweather said.

It was time for the good fairies to give their gifts.

"Your majesties," Flora spoke, bowing to the King and Queen. "Each of us the child may bless, with a single gift, no more, no less."

She waved her wand above the cradle. "Little princess, my gift shall be the gift of beauty."

A vision of a lovely young woman appeared above the cradle. Roses in every shade of purple and pink took shape, filling the throne room with fragrance. The enchanting voices of an invisible chorus sang gently, wishing the Princess hair as golden as sunshine and lips as red as roses.

Flora's lovely vision faded. Now it was Fauna's turn. She bowed to the King and Queen and raised her wand.

"Tiny princess, my gift shall be the gift of song." Images of silver birds flew from her wand. They seemed to soar through a sapphire sky towards a misty castle where a girl sat singing in a window.

It was a lovely vision and a perfect gift. Fauna was very relieved that she had remembered it.

At last, it was Merryweather's turn. She squared her shoulders and stood over the cradle. She'd thought of a hundred perfectly good gifts. Now whatever word she spoke would be the gift she gave. She hoped it was a good one. Merryweather raised her wand.

"Sweet princess, my gift shall be... "

But no one – not even Merryweather herself – would ever know what gift she might have given. For at that moment a gust of icy wind slammed the doors open and shrieked across the throne room, tearing off hats and veils, twisting skirts, and whipping the royal flags and banners. The room grew dark and cold.

The Queen cried out. The King clutched at his robes. Outside, thunder growled and lightning flashed. Shadows filled the room as if the wind had swept them in.

This was no ordinary storm. A thin wisp of green flame rose in the middle of the hall. Tendrils of hissing, evil-smelling smoke crept across the floor like twisted fingers searching for something – or someone. The crowd stared, hypnotized by the rising flames.

Suddenly, Maleficent stepped from the fire. The crowd drew back, murmuring uneasily.

Long black velvet robes swirled around the evil fairy. Her haughty face was framed by a horned headdress, and she held a jewelled staff in her thin hands.

"What does *she* want here?" Merryweather muttered.

Maleficent smiled at the King and Queen, a smile like steel sharpened by anger and hatred.

"Well, well, quite a glittering assemblage, King Stefan," she said. "Royalty, nobility, the gentry, and oh - ha, ha, ha – how quaint ..." Maleficent glanced at the three good fairies, "...even the rabble."

"I really felt quite distressed at not receiving an invitation."

"You weren't wanted," Merryweather blurted out. Fauna and Flora cringed, half expecting Maleficent to turn on Merryweather with scorching fury. Instead, she pretended to be embarrassed.

"Oh, dear, what an awkward situation," Maleficent responded with a chilly calm. "I had hoped it was merely due to some oversight. Well, in that event, I'd best be on my way."

"And to show I bear no ill will, I, too, shall bestow a gift on the child." The three good fairies drew closer to the cradle. They knew Maleficent too well to trust her gifts.

Maleficent struck her staff on the floor. Sparks skittered across the stones. The blows echoed and died in the waiting silence. No one dared speak or move.

"The princess shall indeed grow in grace and beauty, beloved by all who know her."

Merryweather felt icy fingers close around her heart. Flora and Fauna waited, tense and fearful, beside her. Something terrible was about to happen, and they were powerless to stop it.

Darkness poured like smoke from Maleficent's staff, a darkness filled with thousands of bats. They parted like a curtain to reveal a vision of spinning wheels whirling around a young girl. As Maleficent spoke, the girl in the vision reached out.

"But before the sun sets on her sixteenth birthday, she shall prick her finger on the spindle of a spinning wheel...and die!"

"No!" the Queen cried. She ran to the cradle and snatched up her baby.

King Stefan leapt to his feet. "Seize that creature!" he shouted to the guards.

Flames leapt around Maleficent. "Stand back, you fools!" she commanded. The guards froze. A terrified hush fell on the hall. Courtiers edged towards the door, hoping to escape Maleficent's notice and her wrath.

In a rush of flame and smoke, the evil fairy disappeared, but her raven remained, flying above the crowd and peering down with malicious eyes. Once...twice...three times he circled. Then he, too, disappeared.

A deathly silence filled the throne room, broken only by the Queen's soft weeping.

The good fairies blinked as if awakening from a bad dream. They looked at each other. Something had to be done – and quickly! The longer they waited, the more difficult it would be to alter Maleficent's spell in any way.

"Thank the stars I hadn't given my gift to the Princess yet," Merryweather thought.

As usual, Flora was the first to speak. "Don't despair, Your Majesties. Merryweather still has her gift to offer."

The Queen and King looked up hopefully. "Then she can undo this fearful curse?" the King asked.

The fairies shook their heads. That they could not do. Maleficent's powers were too great. But Merryweather could soften it.

"Just do your best, dear," Flora told her.

Merryweather took a deep breath, closed her eyes and concentrated. Let my gift be strong and wise, she thought. Let love guide it.

She raised her wand. A vision of dark clouds appeared. Then a shaft of golden light broke through them and touched the form of a sleeping young woman.

"Sweet princess, if through this wicked witch's trick, a spindle should your finger prick, a ray of hope there still may be in this, the gift I give to thee."

The stream of light grew stronger, conquering the clouds and bathing the throne room in gold.

"Not in death, but just in sleep, the fateful prophecy you'll keep, and from this slumber you shall wake when true love's kiss the spell shall break."

"For true love conquers all," the unseen enchanted chorus sang its message of hope and faith.

Merryweather lowered her wand. She felt weak and dizzy from her effort to counteract the power of Maleficent's spell.

Flora and Fauna put their arms around her. "You did beautifully, dear," Flora whispered.

The King and Queen bowed to her. "Thank you," the Queen whispered. "Your gift is a comfort to us both." She tried to smile, but her voice shook, and silent tears coursed down her pale cheeks.

In spite of Merryweather's gift, King Stefan feared for his daughter's life. He decreed that every spinning wheel in the kingdom should be burned. In every village and town, in every marketplace, farmhouse and cottage, King Stefan's subjects fed their hearth fires with spindles and spinning wheels. For they wanted to do their part to save their little princess.

From the throne room windows, Flora watched the bonfires in the courtyard. She wondered if Maleficent was watching from her mountain stronghold and laughing at this silly spectacle. As if burning a few pieces of wood could stop her!

"Now, come have a nice cup of tea, dear," Fauna waved her wand and a teapot and teacups appeared in mid-air. "I'm sure it'll work out somehow."

"Well, a bonfire won't stop Maleficient," Merryweather said.

"Perhaps if we reason with her," Fauna suggested. "She can't be all bad."

"Oh, yes, she can," Flora replied.

"I'd like to turn her into a fat old hoptoad!" Merryweather said. She waved her wand and conjured a biscuit. There is nothing like a biscuit when you're upset, she thought. Two helped even more.

"You know our magic doesn't work that way," Fauna reminded Merryweather. "It can only do good, dear, and bring joy and happiness."

"Well, that would make me very happy." Merryweather bit a chunk from her cookie, wishing it were Maleficent's hand.

As the eldest fairy by six and one half thousandths of a second, Flora felt she should be the one to come up with an idea.

She paced the room, muttering to herself. Then suddenly she stopped.

"I have it!" she declared. "I'm going to..." She looked around cautiously. "Even the walls have ears," she whispered. "Follow me."

Making themselves tiny, the fairies followed Flora into a carved wooden box and shut the doors. Then Flora proudly announced her idea. She would turn the Princess into a flower.

"Don't you see? A flower can't prick its finger!" she explained. "She'll be perfectly safe."

"Until Maleficent sends a frost," Merryweather said.

Flora frowned. It was true. Maleficent was always ruining her nicest flowers. And Maleficent would expect them to do something like this. But what could three kind-hearted good fairies possibly do against Maleficent's wily, evil cunning?

"She knows everything," Merryweather said. She felt so discouraged, not even another biscuit would help.

"Oh, but she doesn't, dear," Fauna replied. "Maleficent doesn't know anything about love or kindness or the joy of helping others. You know, sometimes I don't think she's really very happy.

"That's it!" Flora exclaimed. "Of course! It's the only thing she can't understand and won't expect! Of course, the King and Queen will object, but when we explain it's the only way..."

Fauna and Merryweather were confused.

"Explain what?" Merryweather asked.

"About the three peasant women raising a foundling child deep in the forest," Flora answered.

"Who are they?" Merryweather asked.

In answer, Flora waved her wand at the three of them. Instantly the three fairies were dressed like simple peasant women. Flora told them her plan. Together, they would raise the baby in the abandoned woodcutter's cottage deep in the woods.

Fauna was delighted, but Merryweather wasn't sure. Caring for a baby sounded very complicated. Of course, they would have their magic wands to help.

Just then, Flora snatched Fauna's wand. "No magic!" she declared. "Better get rid of those wings, too!"

Merryweather was alarmed. "You mean live like mortals? For sixteen years? But we've never done anything without magic!" Merryweather darted around the box, trying to stay out of Flora's reach.

"And that's why Maleficent will never suspect," Flora replied, taking Merryweather's wand and flicking her wand at her wings. Merryweather thumped to the floor. She wiggled her shoulders. They felt empty and lonesome without wings. But if it helped keep the little princess safe, she would learn to live without magic. Gamely, she followed Flora and Fauna out of the box.

Now all they had to do was convince the King and Queen.

At first the King and Queen were against the fairies' idea.

"I don't need to hide my daughter! My soldiers can guard her!" the King declared. "I'll surround the castle with my army. I'll search every man or woman who looks different. I'll send out spies to listen to everything my subjects say. I'll build walls and barricades!"

"I won't see my daughter take her first steps," the Queen wept, "or hear her first words. I won't be the one to comfort her when she's hurt or frightened." Worst of all, she wouldn't know what kind of person her daughter was growing up to be.

But at last, the fairies convinced the King and Queen. They could not fight Maleficent's evil magic with swords or stone walls. This was their daughter's only hope.

King Stefan opened a chest and counted out 192 silver coins, one for every month of the next sixteen years. The fairies carefully divided the coins into three leather bags. Gold coins might arouse someone's suspicion, but the fairies could safely spend one silver coin a month for the things they needed to care for the Princess.

As the castle bells rang midnight, the fairies slipped through the tall castle gates with their tiny, precious bundle.

The King and Queen watched them go. They stood gazing from the castle window long after the gates had closed and their little one had disappeared from view.

Flying down a city street with your wand to light the way was one thing. Merryweather quickly realised that trying to creep along quietly in clumsy, clomping peasant shoes was quite another. Her woolen shawl itched and her thick peasant skirts tangled around her legs. Her shoulders tingled where her wings had been. Being a peasant was very uncomfortable. She hoped she would become used to her disguise soon.

The town was asleep. But here and there, a silhouette appeared in a candlelit window. A mother awake with an ill child? A poet writing of romance? Or one of Maleficent's spies, watching?

No one, not even the kindest, most loyal of King Stefan's subjects must see them. For even the smallest remark – "I saw the strangest thing last night!" might reach Maleficent and ruin their plans.

At the city gates, the fairies crouched in the shadows and waited for the guard to change. Then they darted through the gate and raced down the road to the shadowy edges of the forest. They had made it this far. But there was still a long way to go.

Merryweather peered into the forest. Huge trees as big as the columns of castles and cathedrals stretched as far as she could see. They were so tall, their tops were lost against the dark sky.

"Are you sure you know the way to the cottage?" she asked Flora.

"Well, of course, dear," Flora said. "It's just..." she hesitated. "That way...I think."

But the narrow forest path soon disappeared in drifts of fallen leaves. Without their wands to light the way, the fairies were soon lost. Still they trudged on. Brambles plucked at their skirts and scratched their hands. Cold, damp mist swirled around their feet.

When they passed the same dead tree three times, Merryweather realised the truth. They were lost.

"Oh, fireflies!" she exclaimed. Just then, something soft and furry brushed against her feet. "Eeek!" she exclaimed. "What was that?"

A small red fox stood on the path. It nosed the bundle in Fauna's arms.

"Get away! Get away!" Merryweather scolded.

But Fauna, who loved and understood animals, wasn't alarmed. "She just wants to see the baby," she said, bending down and opening the blanket. Delicately, the fox sniffed the baby's face.

The little princess opened her eyes and gurgled. She grabbed a tuft of red fur in her chubby hand, and to the watching fairies, it seemed that the little animal smiled.

The fox turned and barked sharply.

Seconds later, an enormous white owl glided onto a branch nearby. The fox yipped to the owl. It listened, turning its broad head from side to side to peer at the fairies with gleaming yellow eyes. Then it nodded, spread its wings and flew away, landing on a branch not far ahead.

The fox tugged at Fauna's skirts with its teeth.

"I do believe the fox wants us to follow her and the owl," Fauna said. "I believe they know the way."

"Well, I'm glad someone does," Merryweather replied as they set off.

With the fox and owl as guides, the path grew easier, and the forest no longer seemed so lonely. Occasionally other animals slipped from the underbrush to trot alongside for a bit before quietly disappearing. A chattering rabbit cheered them with silly stories. A squirrel tossed down nuts to eat. And all that night as they walked, a nightingale serenaded them, lulling the Princess with her song.

It was dawn when they finally reached the woodcutter's abandoned cottage.

The fox and owl stopped at the door.

"How can we ever thank you?" Fauna asked. But the owl was already flying away, its wings glowing white in the thin, grey light. The fox was no more than a quick, bright flash of red beneath the trees.

The fairies opened the heavy wooden door and stepped inside. Stale, sour-smelling air greeted them. Spider webs hung like long grey scarves from the ceiling. Dust lay everywhere, turning everything dingy grey, the colour of an old man's beard.

"Oh, my!" Fauna gasped. "Why, it's...it's simply fab–"

"Filthy!" Merryweather interrupted. "It's the dirtiest place I've ever seen. How can we ever hope to raise the Princess, I mean the baby in this?"

"We will because we must," Flora said simply. "It just needs cleaning. I believe humans use hot water, and something they call elbow grease. Did anyone remember to bring any?"

"Soap. They use soap," Merryweather snapped. "I brought some. It's lucky I did, too," she muttered as she dug in her bag. "Elbow grease, indeed!"

"What we need first is a nice hot cup of tea!" Fauna said. She waved her hand in the air. Nothing appeared. "Oh, dear, I forgot," she giggled. "No wands! What do we do now?"

Merryweather lifted a grimy kettle from its hook over the fireplace. "We fill this with water and build a fire," she said.

None of them had ever started a fire without magic, and it took a few burnt fingers and some hot tempers before a fire was warming the cottage and the kettle was singing on the hearth. The baby slept, snugly tucked into a wooden box padded with the fairies' shawls.

Merryweather dug a package of biscuits from her bag and shared them.

"How perfectly clever of you to remember biscuits," Flora praised her.

"Yes," Merryweather agreed, happily helping herself to a second. "I always say, there's no trouble that can't be helped with a biscuit."

All that day and for many more, the fairies scrubbed and dusted, swept and polished. It was more tiring and difficult without their wands than they had ever imagined.

And wetter, too, Merryweather thought as she knocked over the water bucket and soaked her feet for the third time.

She slumped onto a three-legged stool in the corner and began wringing water from the hem of her dripping skirt.

"There's a rather large spider just over your head, dear," Flora pointed out. "You might want to move."

"If anyone moves, it won't be me!" Merryweather stood on the stool and glared at the spider. It glared back with beady yellow eyes.

"Scoot!" Merryweather shouted. "Go on. This isn't your home anymore!"

The spider waved its legs furiously. Merryweather glared harder.

"Grrrr!" she growled.

With a frightened little "eek!" the spider dropped to the floor and scuttled through a crack in the door.

Merryweather sat back down. "How do humans do all this without magic?" she asked.

"Amazing, isn't it?" Flora answered. "And just think, they do it over and over, every day of their lives."

Merryweather sighed. The very thought exhausted her.

**B**ut no matter how tired, sore, gritty, and wet the fairies felt, each time they gazed at the baby princess or held her, the work didn't seem so difficult, after all.

What they couldn't accomplish by magic, their love for her would help them do.

As the months passed, the fairies turned the cottage into a warm, comfortable home. Once a month, they took turns walking to a village far from the woods to spend one silver coin for the things they needed.

Flora planted a garden and spent hours singing to the cabbages. Fauna followed the birds and animals to the best places to pick berries and gather nuts. Merryweather cooked and washed and mended. And they all cared for the baby.

We should give her a new name," Merryweather said one day as she lifted the baby princess, rosy and glowing, from her bath tub. "We mustn't call her Aurora, but we can't go on calling her 'the baby' forever."

"She's as pink and pretty as a rosebud," Flora said. "Perhaps Rose would suit her?"

Just then, the baby giggled, grabbed Merryweather's hair and tugged. "Ouch!" Merryweather laughed as she disentangled the chubby fist.

"Rose is a nice name," Merryweather said. "But our little rose isn't some tame garden rose. She has spirit. She's a little wild rose."

"Wild Rose doesn't sound like a very good name." Fauna thought a moment. "I know – we'll call her Briar Rose."

**B**ut as happy as they were, the fairies never relaxed their vigilance.

Each time one of them went to market, she brought back frightening news about Maleficent. Her goons were searching for the baby princess everywhere. No one knew when or where they would appear. They smashed down doors and crashed through windows. They peered into cradles and overturned beds. They broke open cupboards and rummaged through chests.

"The brutes!" Flora exclaimed. "They're terrifying everyone in the kingdom. No one can stand up to them."

Merryweather felt as if a dark cloud had swept across the sun. "We should have a hiding place for Briar Rose," she said. "Just in case."

Merryweather's suggestion was fortunate. For only a few weeks later, Fauna was leaving the cottage to pick berries when the little fox dashed from the woods. It barked frantically at her, then raced away as if something dreadful was on its trail. Fauna understood at once. Danger was coming. She rushed into the cottage.

"They're coming! Maleficent's goons!" Fauna said. "The fox warned me."

Instantly, the fairies put Merryweather's plan into effect. Fauna took Briar Rose and hurried upstairs to the attic, where they had cut a small trap door out onto the roof. From there, she clambered onto a broad branch where they'd hung a small, secure hammock hidden in the leaves. Fauna climbed in and held Briar Rose close.

"Be very quiet, my darling," she whispered. The baby looked at her as if she understood.

Flora and Merryweather raced around the cottage, stuffing baby blankets, clothes and toys into a sack. They could hear the clank and thud of heavy, armoured feet crashing up the path.

As the goons' fists boomed against the door, Merryweather pulled a flagstone from the floor, crammed the sack inside the hole she'd dug and replaced the stone.

The door shuddered in its frame. Merryweather and Flora braced themselves against it, but they were no match for the goons' strength. The door crashed open, knocking Flora across the room.

Merryweather stood on the flagstone, hiding it beneath her skirts, and shook her mop at the goons. "You're tracking mud on my clean floor!" she shouted. "Is that how your mothers taught you to behave?"

The goons looked surprised. No one ever shouted at them. They were the ones who did the yelling.

"We look for baby princess," the leader growled. "You have?"

Merryweather's heart thudded, but she was determined not to show fear. She laughed.

The lead goon looked puzzled. He scratched his scaly head. No one ever laughed at them. They were scary. "You big dunces," Merryweather snapped.

"Look at us. Two old peasant women. What would we be doing with a baby? If Maleficent hears how stupid you've been, she'll turn you to stone! Why, I almost feel sorry for you. What ugly gargoyles you'll make on Maleficent's castle towers!"

The biggest goon began to shake with fear. "We never tell. You never tell. We go now." The goons edged out the door.

"Oh, no you don't!" Merryweather grabbed the last goon and thrust the mop into his claws. "You're not going anywhere until you've mopped up your filthy tracks. And if you don't do it right now I'm telling Maleficent how stupid you were myself!"

Nearly sobbing with terror, the goon grabbed the mop, sloshed it across the footprints, then ran howling for the woods.

It took three biscuits before Merryweather felt calmer, but Briar Rose was safe for now.

The goons' visit had shaken the fairies, so for a long time they stayed close to the cottage. Every night one of them sat up, watching the woods for any sign of danger. But no one ever bothered them again.

A year passed. Briar Rose learned to walk and toddled everywhere, exploring. She discovered the fun of splashing in rain puddles and digging muddy holes, the sweet taste of strawberries in Fauna's garden and the stingy taste of ants. It took all the fairies' energy just to keep up with her. More than once, Merryweather wished for her wand.

Flora kept a journal of the things Briar Rose said and did. "Someday, when she's grown, she'll want a way to remember this time," Flora said as she pasted a lock of Briar Rose's hair into the journal.

Briar Rose's second birthday passed, then her third and fourth. She was a cheerful, sweet-tempered child. But she was a curious one, too, and sometimes her questions were a bit unsettling.

One day she held up three dolls she'd made from sticks and scraps of cloth. "It's a mama and a papa and a little girl," she told Merryweather. "Why don't I have a mama and papa? All the little forest animals have them."

Merryweather sighed. She and the others had known this question would come someday. But it was still hard to know how to answer. "The animals only have one mama to love them," she answered. "You have three of us, so you're loved three times as much."

Briar Rose clambered into Merryweather's lap. "I love you, too, Aunt Merryweather. And Aunt Flora and Aunt Fauna," she said. "But I still wish I had a mama and a papa."

Merryweather's heart ached as she held the little girl close. "Someday you will, my darling," she whispered. "I promise!"

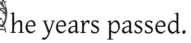he years passed.

Briar Rose turned four, then five and six. She loved the wood and all its creatures and was especially fond of bringing small hurt or orphaned animals home.

One day Flora looked up from the fireplace where she was stirring the soup and sniffed. She smelled...polecat! The sour, musty odour was unmistakeable.

"Aunt Flora, look what I found." Briar Rose stood in the cottage doorway. Her hair was tangled with twigs and leaves. Her dress was torn and wet, and her feet were muddy. Worst of all, she was cradling a baby polecat in her apron.

Briar Rose came to the fireplace, trailing a wave of choking scent. "I found him in the woods. Isn't he cute? His leg is cut. I'm going to make it better."

Flora pinched her nose shut. "Briar Rose, you can't bring a polecat into the house," she said. "You're seven years old. You know better."

"But Aunt Flora, I thought you said we should care for all creatures. It's not his fault he's stinky." Briar Rose's eyes filled with sympathetic tears.

"Very well." Flora sighed. "You can care for him. But not in the cottage. Ask Aunt Merryweather to help you build a pen for him outside."

"But he wants to sleep with me," Briar Rose pouted.

"No arguing," Flora answered. She was glad Briar Rose was kind and loving, but sometimes a fairy simply had to put her foot down.

Perhaps we've let Briar Rose run freely about the woodland too long, she thought. After all, she wouldn't live in the forest forever. It was time they began teaching her how to behave like the princess she was, and would be again someday.

And so, the next evening, the fairies closed and barred the shutters and began Briar Rose's lessons. She liked learning to curtsey to Flora and Fauna. She giggled when Merryweather waltzed her around the room. She didn't even mind walking back and forth with a book balanced on her head for her posture.

But Briar Rose didn't see any reason to learn which fork to use for salad and which for dessert. "We only have one fork and spoon each anyway," she argued as she sat at the table surrounded by every eating utensil in the house.

"Knowing this might be useful to you someday," Flora answered. "And it would make us happy if you'd try to learn."

"All right, Aunt Flora. I'll try," Briar Rose answered. "To make you happy. But I still don't understand why everyday table manners aren't good enough. No one grand is ever going to visit us."

Flora sighed.

It was hard to teach Briar Rose without telling her the real reason for her lessons. She didn't blame the child for thinking it was all a bit silly.

Of all her lessons, Briar Rose loved learning to read and write best. Soon she was begging her aunts to bring her books from the market. On her ninth birthday, Flora gave Briar Rose the journal she'd been keeping and said it was hers to write in from now on.

Briar Rose carried the journal with her everywhere, tucking spring flowers, ferns and bright autumn leaves between the pages where she wrote her thoughts. For though she loved her guardians, like every growing child, Briar Rose had questions and dreams, too, that were hers and hers alone. Questions like "Who am I?" "Why won't my Aunts let me go anywhere?" "Why can't I have any friends?" "What is so frightening about strangers?"

She loved to sit and dream in her favourite spot on a hilltop in the forest. In the distance, she could see a road that looked like a ribbon of silver, leading towards the walls of a city. Above the city walls, castle towers gleamed in the bright air.

She imagined herself walking through the busy market streets, choosing a book or ribbon for her hair. Perhaps the castle gates would open, and the King and Queen would ride out on white horses, surrounded by knights in silver armour.

Someday, I'll go there, Briar Rose thought. Perhaps, I'll see the King and Queen ride by.

Most of all, Briar Rose imagined what it would be like to have a friend to share adventures like those in her books. She loved her aunts and animal friends. But she often thought she'd like someone to talk to and laugh with. Someone who would want to climb trees, wade in streams and explore the forest.

The more she imagined a friend, the more real he became. In her mind she named him Forrest, and she pretended he was with her in the forest. She even wrote about him in her journal as if he were real.

"Forrest and I swung on wild grape vines today." "I'm teaching Forrest to read. He likes stories about knights best." "Forrest and I celebrated his birthday. I gave him one of my books."

She knew that imagining Forrest wasn't the same as having a real friend, but it would have to do.

The fairies watched Briar Rose grow more lovely and loving every year. But they sometimes saw a question flicker across her face like a shadow, and they knew she was wondering about the hidden way they lived.

"Maybe she's old enough to know," Merryweather said one evening after Briar Rose had gone to bed. "She can keep the secret, surely."

"No, dear," Flora shook her head. "Best not to take the chance. She's fifteen. We only have a year to go before Maleficent's spell is broken."

That same afternoon, as Fauna was hunting mushrooms, she overheard Briar Rose talking nearby. Fauna peered through the trees and saw Rose, surrounded by forest animals. "Sometimes I don't know who I really am," she was telling them. "But I suppose that means I can pretend to be anybody." She laughed and the animals chirped and chattered in response.

"Should I be pretend to be the eldest in a family of sixteen children?" she asked the rabbits. They thumped their feet and vehemently shook their heads "no."

"I could pretend be the Queen's lady in waiting. "Yes, Your Majesty, no Your Majesty." She curtsied to a giggling squirrel.

A pair of bluebirds flew to Briar Rose and placed a wreath of honeysuckle and wild roses on her head like a crown.

"Oh, I'm a princess, of course!" she exclaimed. Fauna stifled a little gasp. Had Briar Rose guessed the secret?

Fauna hurried to tell the others. That night, they watched Briar Rose very carefully.

"Is there anything you'd like to tell us about your day, my dear?" Flora asked kindly.

"Yes, anything you might have accidentally discovered?" Merryweather added.

"Well – actually, I did," she answered.

The fairies shot each other horrified looks. But they needn't have worried. For Briar Rose pulled a delicate silver chain with a tiny silver heart from her apron pocket. The locket was tarnished and the links were caked with dirt.

"Where did you find that?" Flora said.

"One of the magpies brought it to me," Briar Rose replied. "I wonder whose it is."

"Oh, it's probably something the magpie found on the road to the market," Flora answered casually.

But the fairies recognised it. It was Princess Aurora's baby locket, lost long ago on their flight into the forest.

Far away in King Hubert's kingdom, Prince Phillip had become a handsome young man with a quick sense of humour and a generous heart.

Every day was packed with lessons, for a prince must know a great deal to become a wise, strong ruler. He learned jousting and fencing, horsemanship and wrestling. There were classes in court etiquette and dancing. He spent long hours with royal tutors learning maths and geography, languages, philosophy, art and music. Sometimes he felt as if his brain would explode.

But as busy as he was, Prince Phillip often found himself wondering about the Princess Aurora. Would she ever be found? What was she like? He hoped she wasn't prissy and vain, or silly and giggly like some of the princesses he'd met. He would have to marry her whether he liked her or not.

It was a gloomy thought. There were times when he wished he didn't have to be a prince and could marry whomever he pleased. But if he wasn't a prince, who would he be?

It all seemed very confusing.

In the lonely castle that should have rung with the happy laughter of a growing child, King Stefan and the Queen waited for the years to pass, and wondered about their daughter, too.

What does she like to do? the Queen wondered as she gazed from her windows. She tried to imagine her daughter. Would she be graceful? Did she like to dance? Did she like pink or blue best? What made her happy?

Is she smart? the King wondered. Would she want to ride horses with him? Would she laugh at his jokes?

As the years passed, the hopes of the King and Queen grew stronger. At last, Princess Aurora's sixteenth birthday drew near.

"Soon," their robes seemed to whisper on the stone castle floors. "Soon," their footsteps echoed the refrain. "Soon...soon...soon. She'll be home soon."

"Soon!" Maleficent screamed at her goons in her castle high in the Forbidden Mountains. "The Princess's sixteenth birthday is tomorrow. You must find her soon!"

The more the mountains thundered with Maleficent's wrath, the more the people of King Stefan's kingdom rejoiced. For they knew it meant her evil prophecy had not yet been fulfilled.

Maleficent's goons watched her fearfully as she paced her gloomy throne room. "Sixteen years and not a trace of her. She couldn't have vanished into thin air," she muttered. She whirled on the goon leader, who flinched.

"Are you sure you searched everywhere?"

"Uhh…yep…yep…everywhere. We searched mountains and, uh forests, and, uh houses." He remembered the cottage in the forest and the old peasant woman who had told him Maleficent would turn him into stone for his stupidity and gulped. "and, uh…all the cradles," he finished.

"Cradles!" Maleficent turned to the raven perched on her throne. "Did you hear that, my pet? All these years, they've been looking for a baby!" Maleficent laughed hysterically.

The foolish goons joined in. But only for a moment.

"Fools! Idiots! Imbeciles!" Maleficent screamed, hurling lightning bolts at them. Screeching, the goons stampeded from the room.

Maleficent collapsed on her throne. "They're hopeless. A disgrace to the forces of evil," she muttered. She stroked her raven's glossy feathers.

"My pet, you are my last hope. Circle far and wide. Search for a maid of sixteen with hair of sunshine gold and lips red as the rose. Go and do not fail me."

The raven blinked its blood-red eyes. Then it silently flew out of throne room window.

In her bedroom in the cottage, Briar Rose heard music.

She was dancing, skimming across a shining floor in the arms of a handsome young man. He was gazing into her eyes. She was...awake.

Briar Rose lay in bed, trying to recapture the floating feeling. It had been such a lovely dream. She'd had it many times, but always woke before it ended.

A warm spring breeze carried the scent of wild roses and honeysuckle inside. A bird sang outside her window. Then she remembered. Today was her birthday – her sixteenth birthday. Was that why she had been feeling so odd lately? As if something was about to change? As if she could hear music playing faintly in the distance?

But no one said "happy birthday" at breakfast. Maybe her aunts had forgotten, Briar Rose thought. Well, she was too grown up to be disappointed if they didn't remember, she told herself. They did so much for her every day. And she had noticed that they had been a little more dithery than usual, almost as if they are thinking about something else.

But of course the fairies had remembered! This was the day they had been dreaming of for so long. To celebrate, they were planning an extra-special surprise. While Briar Rose was upstairs, they huddled over a book of dress patterns.

"This is the one I picked," Flora pointed to a lovely gown.

"We'll make it blue," Merryweather said.

"Oh, no dear. Pink," Flora answered.

Merryweather glowered, but before she could argue, Briar Rose came downstairs.

"What are you three dears up to?" she asked.

The fairies slammed the book shut and hid it behind their backs.

Flora thrust a basket at Briar Rose. "We want you to pick some berries." Merryweather told her. "Lots of berries," Fauna added.

They handed her a shawl and pushed her out the door.

"Now don't hurry back, dear! But don't go too far. And don't speak to strangers." They called confusing directions after her. Briar Rose smiled. Her aunts were odd sometimes, but she loved them with all her heart.

The moment Briar Rose was out of sight, the fairies went to work. Briar Rose would be so surprised!

"A real birthday party," Merryweather said.

"With a real birthday cake," Fauna added.

"Yes, and a dress a princess can be proud of!" Flora said, lifting yards of gleaming satin from a trunk. "I'll get the wands," Merryweather said, starting up the stairs.

Flora stopped her. "No magic," she said. "We're taking no chances."

Merryweather disagreed. The sixteen years would end at sunset. Surely they could use their magic today of all days. Flora had never sewn anything more complicated than a tea towel or apron before. And Fauna had never baked a fancy cake.

But Flora was sure it would all be simple as long as they followed instructions.

Flora shoved Merryweather up on to a stool and draped the satin Fauna had cheerfully measured over her head. Merryweather looked like a giant pink cupcake. Then Flora happily cut an enormous hole in the cloth. "It's got to have a hole in the bottom." she explained.

Merryweather looked at the pile of cloth around her feet. "It's pink!" she exclaimed. "I wanted it blue."

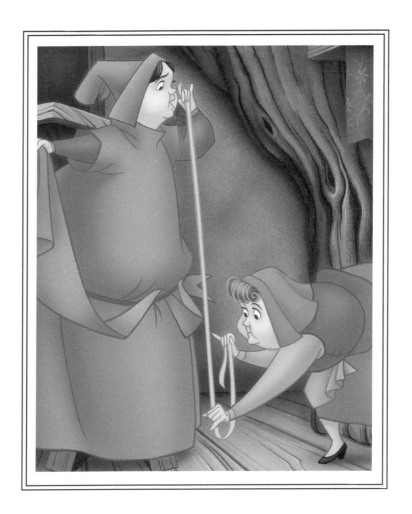

Meanwhile, Fauna cheerfully measured ingredients into a giant bowl. She had always wanted to bake a fancy cake. She planned to make it fifteen layers with pink and blue forget-me-nots.

"Flour, three cups," she read from the book. "Two eggs, fold in gently. Fold?" Looking puzzled, Fauna carefully put the eggs into the batter without breaking them and gently patted the batter over them.

"Now, yeast, one tsp," she continued. "Tsp?"

"One teaspoon," Merryweather muttered from beneath the heaps of cloth draped over her.

The dress looked awful. But Flora was sure it would look much better on Briar Rose.

As the fairies stitched and measured, snipped and stirred, they couldn't help but feel a little sad about how fast the years had flown. "It seems only yesterday we brought her here," Merryweather sniffed.

"Just a tiny baby," Fauna cradled the batter as if it were a baby.

Merryweather began to cry. "After today, she'll be a princess and we won't have any Briar Rose!"

Soon all three of them were sobbing.

"Now, now, now, we all knew this day had to come," Flora tried to sound cheerful. "After all, we've had her for sixteen years." But she knew she'd miss their happy days together in the cottage, too.

Still, there was something wonderful to celebrate. Tonight Rose would finally be free to be what she was always meant to be – a princess.

Which reminded her: They still had a lot to do to finish Briar Rose's surprise. "We're acting like a lot of ninnies!" she exclaimed. "Come on! She'll be back before we get started!"

Briar Rose walked through the woods to a place she knew where the berries grew ripe and sweet in the sun.

The dewy grass felt cool on her bare feet. The air was perfumed by pine and wild roses. Sunlight poured through the trees, so that she seemed to walk through columns of gold.

Birds and little animals flew and ran to greet her. A pair of fluffy brown rabbits hopped out of their hollow log and joined her. A cheeky squirrel raced along a branch and jostled a sleeping owl.

"Who! Who! Who!" the owl called as he woke.

Two bluebirds lit on a nearby branch. Briar Rose listened to them sing together and smiled. But she felt wistful, too. Every animal and bird in the forest had someone to love. If her heart kept singing, would her song reach someone who would find and love her in return? As she sang, Briar Rose's voice wound like a silver thread among the trees.

Not far away, Prince Phillip reined in his horse Samson and looked around at the dense thicket of trees surrounding them. "Well, Samson, you've done it again," Phillip said. "Every time I let you take a short cut, we get lost."

Samson whickered. He was a horse. It wasn't up to him to find the way. But he'd never known a prince who would ask for directions. Phillip just hadn't been paying attention to where they were going.

Samson was right, for Phillip had been deep in thought. He was on his way to King Stefan's castle. Tonight, he would see Princess Aurora for the first time in sixteen years. They would be married, whether they loved each other or not.

Prince Phillip was a brave young man, but now he was nervous. "Maybe we could just stay lost for a few days, eh, Samson?" he joked.

Just then, Briar Rose's voice floated to him on a breeze.

"You hear that, Samson?" Phillip asked. "Beautiful! What is it? Come on. Let's find out."

Samson balked. He'd had enough wandering about. He wanted to find the way to the castle and get to a nice warm stall in the stable.

Phillip patted Samson's neck. "What if I gave you an extra bucket of oats?" he coaxed. "And a few carrots?"

Carrots! Samson's ears pricked up. He adored carrots! With a whinny, he reared, and galloped towards the sound of the voice. He raced under a low-hanging branch and knocked Prince Phillip from his saddle.

Suddenly, Samson realised Phillip wasn't in the saddle. He stopped and looked back.

Phillip glared at him from the middle of a stream. "No carrots for you today, Samson!" The Prince scolded.

Samson hung his head, but Phillip laughed and splashed him. He climbed from the stream, yanked off his boots and poured the water out. Then he pulled off his soggy cape and hat and hung them on a branch to dry.

Prince Phillip lay back on the mossy bank with his hands behind his head to wait for his clothes to dry. He was in no hurry to reach the castle. His whole life would change tonight, and Phillip wasn't sure he was ready. He didn't know why his father thought everything had to be done so quickly. What was the rush to marry the princess? Again, the nagging worry came to him. What if he didn't like her? What if she didn't like him?

Nearby, Briar Rose dabbled her feet in the stream, tossed the petals from a wild rose into the clear, cool water and watched them drift slowly downstream.

"Why do they still treat me like a child?" she asked her animal friends.

"Who?" the owl replied.

"Aunt Flora and Fauna and Merryweather. They never want me to meet anyone."

The birds and forest creatures sympathized.

Again, the strange, restless sensation came over her, as if she were waiting for something to happen. She rose and followed the stream to the edge of the meadow. She sat beneath a tree, and leaned towards her friends.

"But you know something?" she said. "I fooled them. I have met someone."

The rabbits' ears perked up. The birds twittered. Even the squirrels stopped quarrelling over fallen nuts and listened. They all wanted to know more.

"A prince. He's tall and handsome. We walk together and talk together and just before we say goodbye, he takes me in his arms... and then... I wake up."

The animals and birds slumped with disappointment.

"It's only in my dreams. But they say if you dream a thing more than once, it's sure to come true," Briar Rose spoke hopefully. "And I've seen him so many times."

A squirrel scampered closer to Briar Rose. A flash of red in the woods caught his eye, and he scampered through the trees for a closer look. A hat and cape hung dripping from the branch. The little squirrel studied them. He saw the boots on the ground below. He thought about Briar Rose's dream. And he had an idea.

Quick as a wink, he scurried back to the other animals and plunked an acorn at the owl.

"Who? Who?" The owl hooted, looking up.

The squirrel beckoned to him to follow. A bluebird, a cardinal and two rabbits hurried along, as well.

The squirrel put on the hat and scampered off. The two rabbits jumped into the boots and hopped away. The birds flew away holding the cape in their beaks.

Prince Phillip didn't notice. He had his eyes closed and was thinking about the lovely voice he'd heard.

"You know, Samson, there was something strange about that voice. Too beautiful to be real. Maybe it was some mysterious being...a...a wood sprite...or..."

Samson looked up from grazing and whinnied with alarm as he saw Phillip's clothes disappear through the trees.

Phillip jumped up. "Here! Stop!" he shouted.

Samson followed more slowly, still chewing a mouthful of spring grass. It was just common horse sense not to rush lunch. And after all, Phillip couldn't get far without him.

Moments later Briar Rose looked up to see the animals dressed in Prince Phillip's clothes. She wondered where the cape and hat and boots had come from. But everything seemed so strange these days, as if she were always half lost in a dream. Perhaps the clothes were simply part of it

"Why, it's my dream prince," she said.

Briar Rose curtsied to the owl, and he bowed back. The birds wrapped a cloak sleeve around Briar Rose's shoulder as if an invisible prince were holding her in his arms.

"You know, I'm really not supposed to speak to strangers," she said. "But we've met before."

The secret music she had been hearing in her imagination for so many days seemed to grow clearer. "I walked with you, once upon a dream," she sang.

Briar Rose began to waltz. The owl and rabbits hurried to stay in step as she twirled and swayed. Lost in her dream and her song, Briar Rose didn't hear the rustling in a nearby thicket, or see the eyes watching her.

Prince Phillip and Samson peered from their hiding place. Phillip thought he had never seen anyone as lovely. Who was she? He had to know.

Silently, Phillip stepped from his hiding place and stole up behind Briar Rose. He took her hands in his, and began to sing with her.

"Oh!" Briar Rose turned around with a gasp. "Who are...how did...?" She tried to pull away, but Phillip held her hand.

"I'm awfully sorry. I didn't mean to frighten you," he said.

"It's just that you're a...a..." She lowered her eyes.

"A stranger?" Phillip finished her sentence. "But don't you remember? We've met before. You said so yourself. Once upon a dream."

They looked into each other's eyes, and as simply and quickly as that, they both knew. It was as if, alone in their own worlds, each had been waiting for the other to appear.

All day, Briar Rose and Phillip walked and talked together.

The hours passed in a golden haze woven with the scent of roses, the soft touch of spring breezes, and the trill of meadowlarks. And running through everything they said or did was the joyful singing in their own hearts. It was as if there were only the two of them, walking and talking in a dream they shared.

But all dreamers must awaken sometime.

As Briar Rose and Prince Phillip stood in her favourite spot overlooking the castle, Prince Phillip gazed at her curiously.

"Who are you? What's your name?" he asked.

Briar Rose startled as if awakened suddenly. "Oh , no! No, I can't, I..." She pulled her hand from Phillip's and ran towards the forest, suddenly as startled and wary as a faun.

"But when will I see you again?" Phillip called.

"Oh, never! Never! Well, maybe someday!" Briar Rose answered as she disappeared into the trees. "This evening," she called. "At the cottage in the glen."

The day had not been quite as wonderful for the fairies.

The cottage was a shambles. Scraps of fabric, pins and thread littered the floor, which was coated with flour and sugar. The fairies were hot, sticky and dishevelled. Surprises were not the easiest things to pull off.

"Well, what do you think of it?" Fauna asked as she lit sixteen candles on a wobbling blue cakey tower on the table.

Merryweather raised one skeptical eyebrow.

"It will be much stiffer after it's baked," Fauna explained. She jammed a broom handle into the collapsing dough.

Flora tugged at the gown Merryweather was modelling. "What do you think of the dress?" she asked.

Merryweather looked at it. The neck was lopsided, the long floppy sleeves barely hung on. Bows flapped loosely here and there. The skirt was bunched and crooked, and the hem went sometimes southways, sometimes northways and every which way the rest of the time.

Merryweather glowered. She shrugged her shoulders and the dress fell to pieces around her feet. "I think we've had enough of this nonsense." she stated. "I think we ought to think of Rose and what she'll think of this mess." She hopped from the stool and marched towards the stairs, scattering pins behind her. "I still think what I thunk before. I'm going to get those wands."

Flora and Fauna looked at the cake, the dress and each other. Merryweather was right. Quickly they locked the door, closed the windows and plugged up every crack and cranny with rags. They couldn't take any chance that the tiniest sparkle of the magic from their wands might escape.

But they forgot to close the fireplace damper.

Merryweather clattered downstairs with the wands. "Here they are, good as new!" she said, looking at hers fondly. She hoped it hadn't grown rusty or creaky from disuse. "Oh, how I've missed you," she told it. The wand gave a happy little sigh and snuggled into her hand as if it had missed her, too.

"Now, you take care of the cake," Flora told Fauna.

Merryweather pointed her wand at the fabric. "While I..." she started.

"Clean up the room," Flora told her. "And I'll make the dress."

Merryweather frowned. Here she was, using her wand for the first time in simply ages and she wanted to do something more fun than housework! But what really mattered was having everything perfect for Briar Rose, so she shrugged and pointed her wand at the broom.

"Mop, broom, Flora says clean up the room." The broom began to sweep. The mop dipped itself into the bucket and sloshed water across the floor.

"Eggs, flour, milk," Fauna chanted. "Just do it like it says here in the book. I'll put on the candles." The flour, eggs and milk poured themselves into a mixing bowl, while a spoon stirred merrily.

Flora pointed her wand at the fabric. "And now to make a lovely dress, fit to grace a fair princess."

Snip went the scissors! Flash went the needle as it darted in and out of the fabric.

Merryweather was dancing across the room with the mop when when she saw the dress. "Oh, no! Not pink!" She pointed her wand at the gown. "Make it blue." A sparkle of blue magic streaked up a ribbon and changed the gown to blue. Merryweather danced away.

"Merryweather!" Flora exclaimed. She pointed her wand at the dress. "Make it pink!"

"Make it blue!" "Make it pink!" Flora and Merryweather duelled back and forth across the room, shooting pink and blue magic sparkles at the dress and each other. Streaks of magic zinged and zipped everywhere. They bounced off the pots and pans, ricocheted into the fireplace and shot from the chimney in sparkling pink and blue puffs.

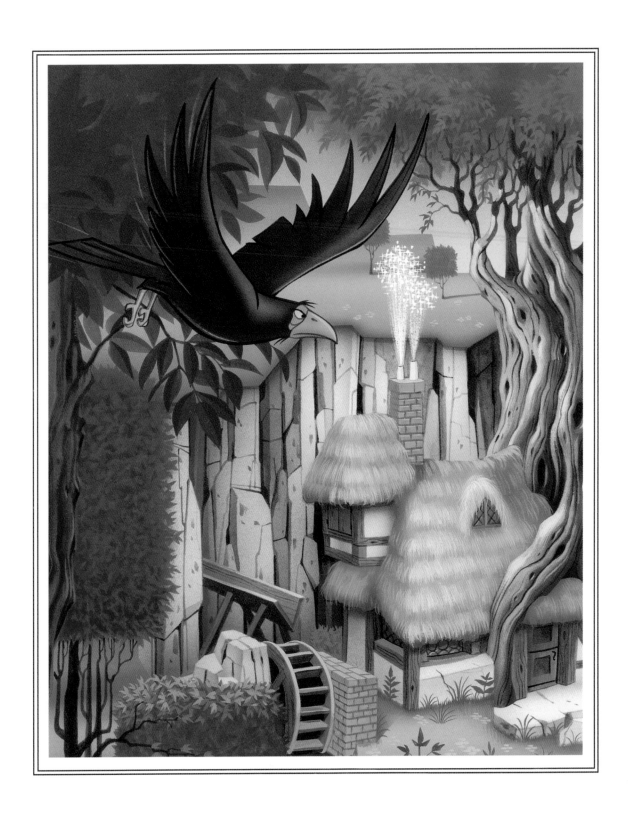

igh overhead, Maleficient's raven flew past, searching for the Princess.

Sparkles erupting from the chimney caught his eye and he dove towards the cottage for a closer look.

Inside the cottage, the fairies heard Briar Rose singing as she approached. "Enough of this foolishness!" Flora said with a final shot of pink sparkles at the dress. Fauna lit the candles on the cake. Merryweather turned off the mop.

Giggling with anticipation, the fairies hid. They could hardly wait to see the look on Briar Rose's face when she saw the gown and cake, and they told her who she really was. It would be the most wonderful day of her life. Briar Rose would have the happiness she deserved.

"Our Rose, a princess at last," Merryweather whispered softly.

"Surprise! Surprise!" the fairies shouted as they popped from hiding when Briar Rose came in.

"Oh, you darlings! This is the happiest day of my life!" Briar Rose exclaimed. "Everything's so wonderful. Just wait till you meet him."

The fairies looked at each other with alarm. "You've...you've met some stranger?" Flora asked.

"Oh, he's not a stranger. We've met before. Once upon a dream." Briar Rose danced around them in slow, dreamy circles.

The fairies were horrified. Briar Rose was in love. It was the worst disaster imaginable. They gathered around their beautiful, beloved girl, knowing that what they were about to say would break her heart.

"You're already betrothed. Since the day you were born. To Prince Phillip, dear," Flora told her.

Briar Rose didn't believe them. "How could I marry a prince? I'd have to be..." She stopped as the realisation swept over her.

"Princess Aurora," Flora said.

All the joy had gone from the cottage.

"Tonight we're taking you back to your father, King Stefan," Flora told her. "You must never see that young man again."

"No! Oh, no!" Briar Rose ran to her room and flung herself on her bed.

The fairies stood in the dim, quiet kitchen, listening to Briar Rose crying. "And we thought she'd be so happy," Merryweather said.

No one saw the raven listening outside the window or heard the sweep of his powerful dark wings as he sped through the darkening sky towards Maleficent's castle.

In her chambers, the Queen watched the sun drop behind the castle towers.

Aurora was coming home. What would she say to her?

In the candlelit banquet hall, King Stefan paced, too. Aurora should be arriving any moment now. These last few hours of waiting seemed as long as all the previous sixteen years combined. What would he say to her?

King Stefan looked at the feast on the table. He couldn't possibly choke down a single bite.

How could King Hubert sit calmly eating as if nothing was happening – as if he hadn't a care in the world?

"Come, man! Buck up!" Hubert shouted. "Battle's over, girl's as good as here." He poured King Stefan a goblet of wine. "Tonight we toast the future!"

The two kings raised their goblets.

Hubert couldn't imagine that Aurora wouldn't adore his Phillip. Why, Hubert himself had already built a castle for them. He could imagine playing with his grandson or dancing with his granddaughter. What could possibly go wrong?

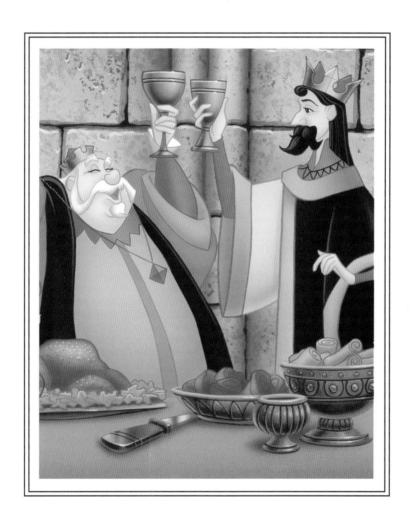

At that moment, trumpets blared.

"His royal highness, Prince Phillip!" A herald's voice rang out.

Hubert raced into the courtyard to meet Phillip. "Hurry, boy! Hurry!" he shouted. "Change into something suitable. Can't have you meeting your future bride looking like that!"

Phillip jumped from the saddle and lifted his father off his feet. "I have met her, Father!" he declared, dancing his loudly protesting father around the courtyard. "Once upon a dream."

"What's all this dream nonsense?" Hubert huffed as Phillip put him down. He tugged his tunic and straightened his crown.

"It wasn't a dream, Father," Phillip answered. "I really did meet her."

"The Princess Aurora? Good heavens! We must tell Stefan."

Phillip stopped him. This was the hard part. King Hubert was not going to be happy. But Phillip hoped his father would accept his choice in time.

"I, I didn't say it was Aurora," Phillip explained. "I said I met the girl I was going to marry."

King Hubert scowled. His brow furrowed and his face turned red.

Phillip took a deep breath and forged ahead. "I don't know who she was. A peasant girl, I suppose."

He counted the seconds, waiting for the explosion he knew was coming. One...two...

"You're JOKING! I won't have it! You're a prince and you're going to marry a princess." Hubert sputtered and spluttered so hard his crown flew off and clattered across the courtyard. Phillip calmly picked it up, brushed it off and handed it back.

"Now, Father, you're living in the past. This is the fourteenth century. Nowadays –"

"Nowadays I'm still the king, and I command you to come to your senses..."

"...and marry the girl I love!" Phillip called as he jumped back into the saddle and galloped Samson towards the castle gates. He'd said what he had to say and was still in one piece. Now he had the most important appointment of his life to keep.

King Hubert sagged like a popped balloon, and he slumped onto a step, holding his head in his hands. "How will I ever tell Stefan?" he muttered.

The sun was setting, and the sky was awash with pale streaks of orange and lavender and dusting the topmost branches of the trees with rosy gold as the three fairies led Briar Rose from the cottage.

We must think of her as Princess Aurora now, Merryweather reminded herself. The poor dear.

The tree trunks stood deep in shadow as they walked along the path. On either side of the path, Briar Rose's forest friends gathered to watch her pass. Squirrels lowered their bushy tails, rabbits bent their ears to honour her. A white owl flew before them. Merryweather thought she glimpsed the gleaming green eyes of the little fox who had helped them so many years ago.

The fairies had kept Briar Rose hidden for so long. Soon she would be safe from harm. They still worried. Would she be happy?

Briar Rose's face was as pale and expressionless as the rising moon. She walked blindly without seeing or caring where she was going. The one thing she had dreamt of all her life had come to her in an afternoon and been snatched away by evening. It didn't matter what she wanted. She had no choice. She was like a prisoner sentenced to life in a dungeon.

No one spoke. The only sound was the rustle of their feet in the fallen leaves, and the sighing of the wind in the trees. A night bird called plaintively in the distance.

"Fare thee well, Briar Rose," Merryweather thought it was saying. "Fare thee well." Merryweather thought the sound would break her heart.

Cautiously, carefully, the fairies led the silent princess through a secret door in the castle walls. This was the time of greatest peril. No one, not even the king and queen, must know that the princess was in the castle until the last possible moment. For until the sun set completely, Maleficent still had time to make her evil curse come true.

They hurried across the shadowy courtyard, ducked through a low door into a tower and slipped into a small room. The fairies bolted the door, drew the curtains, and led Briar Rose to a carved wooden bench before a mirror.

Then they waved their wands.

A crown appeared and Flora plucked the gleaming gold circlet from the air. "This one last gift, dear child, for thee, the symbol of thy royalty." She spoke reverently as she placed the crown on Briar Rose's head. "A crown to wear in grace and beauty as is thy right – and royal duty."

Royal duty. Briar Rose gazed at her reflection. A stranger gazed back at her. What was she doing wearing a crown? All those years, she had wondered who she was, and now she knew. And how she wished oh, how she wished she did not.

She began to cry.

"Let her have a few moments alone," Flora whispered.

With aching hearts, the fairies left the room.

When they were gone, a wisp of pale green smoke rose from the fireplace and drifted towards Briar Rose. She heard strange sounds whispering in the room, like thin high voices calling, "Come... come..."

A cold draft blew from the fireplace, tainted with the smell of damp, mouldy stone and dead ashes. Briar Rose shivered and tried to shut the voices out, but they crept into her mind, blurring her thoughts. She tried to call out to her aunts, but no words came.

The green smoke wound into a glowing ball that floated before her. She couldn't take her eyes from it.

Briar Rose stood slowly and began to follow it. Suddenly a narrow stone stairway opened in the fireplace wall.

Like a sleepwalker, powerless to awaken, Briar Rose stepped into the fireplace and followed the glowing orb up the stairs. Behind her, the wall closed.

In the hallway, the fairies felt the air grow chill and heard a strange whispering sound.

A smoky light glowed from the crack beneath the door.

"Maleficent!" Flora exclaimed.

"Rose! Rose! Rose!" The fairies burst into the room calling her name. But she was gone.

High in the tower, Maleficent listened to the fairies' shouts and smiled.

Flora pointed her wand at the fireplace wall, and it opened again. Frantic, the fairies hurried up the stone steps, calling for Briar Rose.

She heard them, but couldn't stop or turn around. Something was pulling her up the stairs. Briar Rose thought she heard someone shouting. The voices and the name they were calling seemed vaguely familiar. Who is Briar Rose? she wondered. She felt as if she should know. But she couldn't quite recall. Her feet moved of their own accord, carrying her up the stairs, through an archway and into a shadowy room.

In the centre, the globe of light flashed and spun, transforming into a spinning wheel and spindle.

Briar Rose walked towards the spindle. She had never seen anything like it. She wondered what it was.

Maleficent watched Briar Rose approach. Her victory had come at last. No one could defeat her. I control them all, she thought.

"Touch the spindle!" she commanded.

"Rose! Rose! Don't touch anything!"

Briar Rose heard the familiar voices again. But the spindle gleamed so brightly. She longed to touch it.

"No! Don't touch anything!" The voices were nearer now. She hesitated.

"Touch it, I say!" Maleficent's voice was fierce. Obediently, Briar Rose stretched out her hand.

"Rose! Rose!" The fairies' cry was the last thing she heard as the spindle pricked her finger.

The fairies rushed into the room.

Maleficent greeted them with a sneer. "You poor, simple fools, thinking you could defeat me! Me! The mistress of all evil!" She snarled. "Well, here's your precious princess."

She drew back her robes. Briar Rose lay in a pool of light cast by the setting sun.

With a hideous laugh, Maleficent disappeared in a burst of flame.

The fairies took no notice. They knelt and wept beside Briar Rose.

Outside, the light faded and the sun went down.

In the throne room, King Stefan and the Queen waited.

The setting sun gilded their crowns and thrones, but their faces were alight with something far brighter.

Hope.

The Queen's hands trembled with anticipation. Soon, she would hold her daughter.

King Stefan stared at the grand staircase, willing Aurora to appear.

King Hubert bustled into the throne room and plunked down beside Stefan. He cleared his throat nervously. "Stefan, th-there's, there's something important I have to tell you. It's about Phillip."

Just then, the herald cried, "The sun has set. Make ready to welcome your princess."

King Stefan and the Queen clasped hands. "My lovely queen," King Stefan whispered. "Our daughter is home at last."

igh in a tower overlooking the courtyard, the fairies laid the sleeping princess on a bed.

Their hot tears fell on her silken coverlet. They stroked her hair and hands and watched her breathing, lost deep in her dreamless sleep.

Oh, how I wish I hadn't added that part about true love's kiss when I gave my gift, Merryweather thought bitterly. What if her true love never comes, and she sleeps forever? Merryweather wished she had made it someone else's kiss instead, a mother's, a father's, or even an aunt's.

The herald's cry brought the fairies to the balcony. Fireworks exploded above the towers, showering them with gold and silver, pink, blue, red and green. A cheer went up from the courtyard as people prepared to welcome their princess.

"Poor King Stefan and the Queen," Fauna said. "They'll be heartbroken when they find out." Merryweather sighed.

Flora wiped her eyes and squared her shoulders.

Once, again, she was the one who had to come up with a plan. "They're not going to," she announced. "We'll put them all to sleep until Rose awakens." She explained, drawing the velvet curtains around Briar Rose's bed.

Then, making themselves no larger than a firefly's spark, the three fairies flew from the tower and began to touch everyone and everything with a sleeping spell while enchanted voices filled the twilight with a soft song.

The soldiers by the gates closed their eyes and dropped their swords and bows. The scullery maid smiled and nodded off. Knights and their horses, nobles and ladies in their fine clothes, serving men, stable boys and laundresses fell asleep where they stood. Dogs dozed off while scratching their fleas, and even the fleas fell asleep.

All the fires in the castle went out with a sigh. Banners and flags drooped and grew still. The courtyard fountain stopped flowing. One last drop of water plinked into the pond. Then all was silent.

The fairies flew into the throne room. Merryweather snuffed out the candles and Fauna silenced the musicians, while Flora spread her sleeping dust over King Stefan and the Queen.

They fell asleep gazing towards the grand staircase. King Hubert kept talking between enormous yawns.

"Just been talking to Phillip. Seems he's fallen in love with some peasant girl," he muttered.

Flora stopped in mid-flight and hovered near Hubert's large red ear.

"The peasant girl? Who is she? Where did he meet her?" she prompted, resisting the urge to poke him with her wand.

"Just some peasant girl he met...once upon a dream." He began to snore.

Suddenly Flora understood everything. "Once upon a dream? Rose! Prince Phillip!" she exclaimed. "Come on!" she called to Fauna and Merryweather. "We've got to get back to the cottage!"

Phillip felt giddy with happiness as he rode to the woodcutter's cottage.

He planned to ask for the peasant girl's hand in marriage that very night. He was truly sorry about Princess Aurora. He hoped she would understand that he'd had no choice. The gift of true love was not something to throw away, betrothal to a princess or not.

Samson whinnied nervously. It was too quiet. No small creatures rustled in the undergrowth. No owls called or nightingales sang. It was as if every animal was hiding from something. But Phillip was too caught up in his dreams to notice.

The woodcutter's cottage was dark when Phillip arrived, but the door swung open. He stepped inside.

Suddenly the shadows came to life and Maleficent's goons sprang from every corner, grunting and growling.

Phillip smelled the thick stink of unwashed bodies and filthy clothes. Huge scaly hands grabbed his arms and legs. Thick fists hammered his chest and shoulders. Claws jabbed at his face, tore at his cloak and hat and yanked his hair.

Phillip fought, but there were just too many of them. Within moments, he was bound and looking up at Maleficent. She smiled with malicious delight.

"Well, this is a pleasant surprise," she said. "I set my trap for a peasant and, lo, I catch a prince. Away with him. But gently, my pets. I have plans for our royal guest."

The fairies flew on through the wood.

If they could only find Phillip and bring him safely to the castle, Maleficent's spell would end like a bad dream.

But the moment they stepped inside the cottage, they knew they were too late. Furniture lay overturned and splintered. Broken crockery and shattered glass crunched beneath their feet. The shutters hung from their hinges. Briar Rose's birthday cake was smashed, and clawed footprints tracked pink and blue icing across the floor.

Maleficent and her goons had been there. Flora held up a battered hat.

"She's got Prince Phillip!" Merryweather exclaimed.

"At the Forbidden Mountain." Flora said.

"But we can't go there!" Fauna said, her voice trembling.

They were so small, how could they hope to battle Maleficent's powerful evil? They looked at each other. They had to try.

Everyone else was sleeping. They were Briar Rose's only hope. If they could not free Prince Phillip, she would sleep forever.

Flora spoke at last, and though her voice shook, her firmness gave Fauna and Merryweather courage..

"We can, and we must!" she said.

**M**alificent's castle loomed at the top of the Forbidden Mountains.

Black clouds clung to its towers. Dank fog swirled around its foundations. Red lights gleamed from the windows like the glaring eyes of a huge black monster crouched and watching.

The three fairies shuddered as they crept towards the massive drawbridge. A goon marched past. The fairies ducked behind a boulder and waited until his footsteps grew fainter. Then, making themselves tiny, they dashed up the drawbridge chain and squeezed through the hole where the chain came through the stone wall. They were inside.

Maleficent's castle was more terrifying than they'd ever imagined, even in their darkest nightmares. It was a maze of walls and archways, stairs and tunnels. How would they ever find Prince Phillip?

Another goon guard thumped and clanked past, and the fairies squeezed into a crack in the wall to hide. When the goon had passed, they darted out.

"Eek!" Fauna shrieked as they nearly bumped into a sleeping goon. They whirled around and flew into the leering face of a stone gargoyle. Whichever way they turned, the grimacing creatures surrounded them. They seemed so real, the fairies could almost hear them snarl through their bared fangs.

Merryweather shuddered. Their hard, cold eyes seemed to be watching her. She hoped they didn't come to life and begin to howl.

The fairies heard beating drums and wild, hoarse chanting coming from a window above them. They flew to a ledge and peered inside.

In the room below, the goons howled and chanted as they leapt and stomped around a blazing fire that cast blood-red light on their grimacing faces. Shadows writhed across the floor and crawled up the walls. Thick smoke wound around them so that sometimes only an arm or leg was visible, as if it had become detached from its owner and was moving on its own.

Maleficent sat on her stone dais watching the frenzy. The raven sat beside her. "What a pity Prince Phillip can't be here to enjoy the celebration," she said, stroking its wings. "Come! We must go to the dungeon and cheer him up."

The fairies followed as Maleficent glided silently along the dark corridors of her castle and down the damp steps to the dungeon.

Moisture oozed from the stone walls, leaving trails of slime. Small things rustled in the shadows. The raven swooped at something hunched in a corner. It shrieked in terror and scuttled away.

Peeking through an iron-barred window, the fairies saw Maleficent open a heavy door.

Inside a narrow cell, Prince Phillip slumped on a stone bench. His arms and legs were chained. He didn't look up as Maleficent entered.

"Oh, come now, Prince Phillip, why so melancholy?" she taunted him. "A wondrous future lies before you. You, the destined hero of a charming fairy tale come true."

A vision began to form in the dim light of the dungeon. "Behold King Stefan's castle and in yonder topmost tower, dreaming of her true love, the Princess Aurora. But see the gracious whim of fate. Why, 'tis the selfsame maid who won the heart of our noble prince but yesterday."

Phillip's head went up, and hope flared in his eyes. Was it possible? The girl he loved and Princess Aurora were the same? But his eyes grew dull again. What good did knowing do him now?

Maleficent savoured his despair.

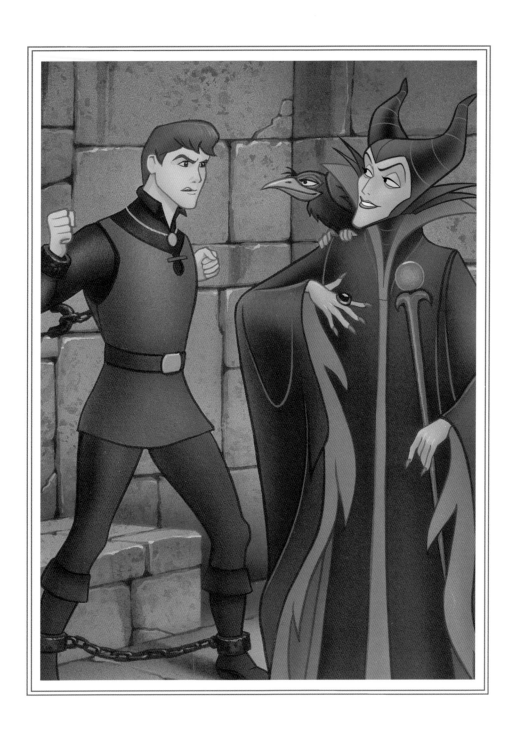

She is indeed most wondrous fair. In ageless sleep, she finds repose. The years roll by, but a hundred years to a steadfast heart are but a day."

The vision of the castle transformed, and as Maleficent continued, Phillip saw himself, decrepit with age, robbed of youth and strength and bowed from years of captivity.

"And now the gates of the dungeon part, and our prince is free to go his way. Off he rides on his noble steed, a valiant figure, straight and tall, to wake his love with love's first kiss and prove that true love conquers all."

Maleficent's laugh was like iron striking stone.

Phillip jumped up, straining against the chains that held him.

Outside the window, Merryweather shook her fists. "Why, you..." she muttered.

"Come, my pet," Maleficent held out her hand to the raven.

The raven peered suspiciously at the window just as Flora pulled Merryweather out of sight.

Inside the cell, Phillip sat in darkness. "Think! Think!" he told himself. "There must be a way to escape!" But when he yanked on the chains, they only bit more deeply into his legs and wrists.

Three pale spots of pink, blue and green light flitted through the window. Phillip blinked. Was he seeing things? The lights grew, illuminating the cell and revealing...

"Fairies!" Phillip exclaimed. "Who are...how did..."

Flora shushed him and began to burn the shackles from his wrists with her wand. Flora went to work on his ankles. The iron glowed white hot. Phillip grimaced as it scorched his skin. At last the manacles snapped. The chains rattled to the floor.

He was free.

Phillip sprang to his feet, but Flora stopped him.

"Wait! The road to true love may be barred by still more dangers which you alone will have to face." She pointed her wand. "So arm thyself with this enchanted shield of virtue and this mighty sword of truth. For these weapons of righteousness will triumph over evil."

A shield appeared on Phillip's arm and a sword sprang to his hand. He held it up, admiring the flash of light along the long, sharp blade.

"Now come, we must hurry," Flora commanded.

They eased the door open – and stared into the raven's cold eyes! It flew up the dungeon stairs, screeching the alarm. Seconds later, Maleficent's goons were thundering towards them.

Phillip and the fairies turned and raced in the opposite direction. They reached a small window. The fairies darted through. As the goons snatched at Phillip's legs and arms, he kicked them away, jumped to the window ledge and threw himself out.

Phillip fell hard, landing on a stinking rubbish heap, and careened down piles of debris. As he landed in the courtyard, the goons howled with rage.

"Phillip, watch out!" Flora shouted as the goons hurled boulders from the ledge. Phillip ducked as one slammed past him and buried itself in the earth of the courtyard. Flora drew her wand and shot magic at the falling rocks.

Poof! They turned into flowers that fluttered and danced in mid-air.

Merryweather and Fauna hurried to Samson and began to use their wands to burn the shackles from his legs.

Screaming with fury, the goons drew their bows. Arrows whined like maddened wasps towards Phillip.

Once again, Flora shot her magic and the arrows turned to flowers. The raven screeched with frustration, and the goons shook their fists and shrieked with anger.

At that moment, the chains fell away from Samson's legs. Phillip leaped into the saddle and raced for the drawbridge.

But the goons would not be easily beaten. Their hatred of Phillip was great. And their fear of Maleficent's wrath was greater. As the raven circled above them, the goons poured rivers of boiling oil over the wall.

Once again, Flora shot magic from her wand. The scalding oil became a rainbow. Phillip and Samson galloped beneath it.

The fairies flew beside him. If Phillip could only make it past the drawbridge, he would be free. But Merryweather saw the raven speeding towards the throne room to alert Maleficent.

Merryweather knew something had to be done about that bird, and she was the fairy to do it. She streaked after it. "When I'm finished with you," she muttered, "there won't be enough left to make a feather duster!"

Merryweather aimed her wand and shot once, twice, three times. Zing! Zing! Zing! But the raven saw her magic coming, and dodged away.

Under archways, up stairs, across battlements and around gargoyles, Merryweather chased the raven. It flew around a tower. Merryweather stopped and hovered in place.

When the evil bird reappeared on the other side, she was waiting. Zing! Merryweather fired her wand. The raven squawked once, and turned to stone.

Maleficent heard the noise, and stormed onto the balcony.

Her eyes fell on her stone pet. "No! Oh, no!" she gasped.

Below her, Phillip galloped Samson up the rising drawbridge, reached the edge and catapulted into space. They landed on the crumbling edge of a cliff. Stones rattled beneath Samson's hooves and crashed into the abyss below. Flanks heaving and straining, Samson scrambled for solid ground, found it – and pounded down the mountain.

Clouds swarmed darkly behind Maleficent as she raised her arms.

A lightning bolt sprang from her hands. She hurled it like a spear at a stone arch. It crashed around Phillip as he galloped through.

Again and again, Maleficent hurled her bolts, blasting gaping holes in the earth, flinging rock through the air, singeing trees, setting bushes aflame.

Sliding in loose rock, plunging over crevices, rearing and leaping over burning trees that crashed in their path, Phillip and Samson galloped down the mountain. There was no time to plan or think. Phillip's mind was empty of everything except his need to escape Maleficent's wrath, and reach the Princess.

"Hurry, Phillip! Hurry!"

The fairies flew alongside, urging him on. At last they reached the bottom of the mountain. A wide, dark plain stretched between them and the castle where the Princess slept.

"Come on, Samson," Phillip urged. "Come on, old friend. We must not lose this race."

Samson's chest heaved. His flanks were covered with foam. But for Phillip, he would run until his heart burst.

Nothing on earth, however, could outrun Maleficent's fury. Maleficent raised her staff skyward. "A forest of thorns shall be his tomb," she chanted. Black clouds swirled around her head. Flashes of lightning illuminated her.

"Borne through the skies on a fog of doom, now go with a curse and serve me well. 'Round Stefan's castle cast my spell!" Maleficent's voice rang through the darkness.

The clouds, whirling faster, turned into a spinning whirlwind of thorns. An evil green light swept across their jagged edges. A howling wheel drove them across the sky.

Shards of lightning struck the earth around Phillip, to the right...to the left...behind him...in front of him.

Each place a lightning bolt struck, the earth split apart and massive thorny vines erupted. They thrust upwards, climbing up each other, winding and twisting themselves into impenetrable knots.

In seconds, Phillip was surrounded by a dense forest of deadly thorns. And still the vines rose, blocking the road, covering the castle gates, crawling up walls and towers until they swallowed everything.

Samson reared and snorted in panic, but Phillip drew his sword and slashed at the thorns.

"This way, Phillip! This way!"

The fairies guided him through the tangled, treacherous maze. The vines were thick as tree trunks, their thorns sharp as daggers. They dug into Phillip's hands and ripped his clothes, raked his arms and face and stabbed through his boots. Still, he hacked and chopped and slashed.

His arms and shoulders burned. His chest ached for air. Again and again, he brought the sword down across the thorns. It felt heavier each time he swung it.

Still, he persisted.

The forest of thorns seemed to go on forever. Phillip began to think that he would be trapped inside. But finally the last vine collapsed beneath his blade. He had made it through.

"No!" Maleficent screamed from her watchtower. "It cannot be!" Flames leapt around her, and she shot from the tower, whirling towards the castle in a fury of fire and smoke.

"Now you shall deal with me, oh Prince, and all the powers of hell!" Maleficent cried as she landed before Phillip.

With an explosion more violent than a thousand furious volcanoes erupting, Maleficent rose up and up in fountains of roaring flame as she transformed into a dragon so huge it blocked the sky.

The dragon's scales were like iron, its claws as long as Phillip's arms, and its yellow eyes glowed with hatred. Its long neck coiled with menace as it reared and lunged, snapping enormous fanged jaws at Phillip.

Streams of fire shot towards him. Burning air seared his lungs. Embers blistered his hands and face. Hot sparks stung his eyes and scorched his cape.

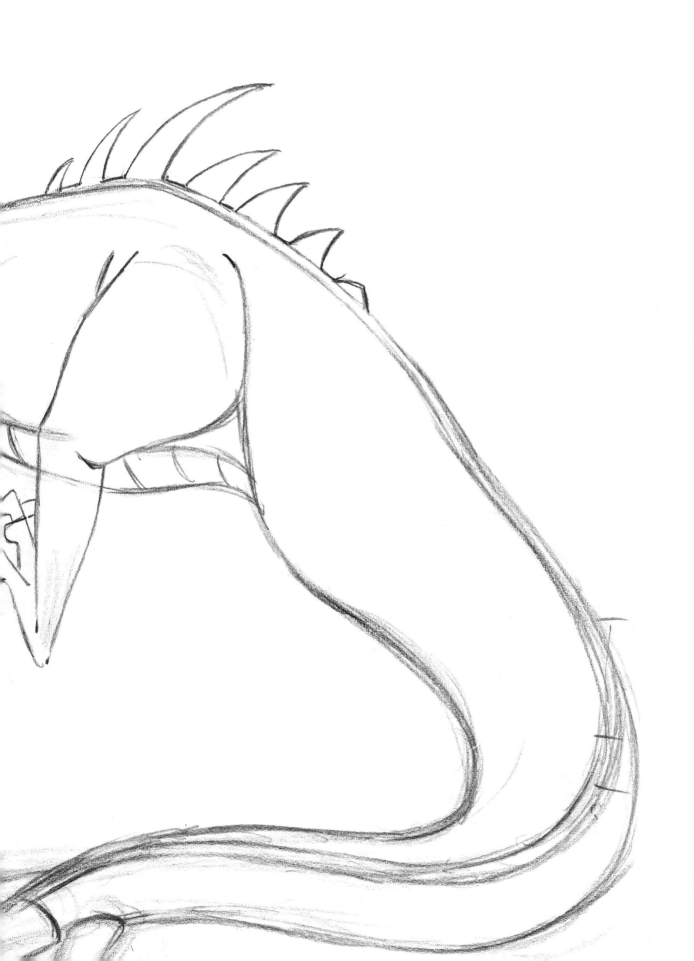

Raising his shield against the flames, Phillip charged.

The dragon lunged again, spitting gouts of flame. The beast's huge head swayed above Phillip, its evil eyes locked on him as it struck again and again. Phillip ducked and dodged, but flames leapt up on every side. The dragon pressed him back, step by step, until he was pinned against a cliff. He could feel the heat from its stones searing his back.

"Up! Up this way!" Flora shouted from the top of the cliff.

Barely able to see through the smoke, gasping for breath, arms and legs trembling with exhaustion, Phillip dragged himself upwards, scrabbling for handholds in the rocky ledges, grasping blasted shrubs with his blistered hands.

As he reached the top, the dragon rose, towering above him.

The fairies watched in horror as it attacked, pressing Phillip towards the precipice. A river of flame roared over him and he dropped his shield. It caught fire and hurtled like a flaming meteor into the inky darkness far below.

Prince Phillip had only his sword now.

The fairies flew to him, and Flora touched it with her wand.

"Now, sword of truth, fly swift and sure, that evil die and good endure!" she commanded. White light rippled along the sword's edges.

One last time, the dragon reared, gathering its furious strength for the final stroke. It lunged. Phillip hurled the sword. It flashed through the air and buried itself in the dragon's heart.

With a roar of fury, the dragon fell. Its snapping jaws barely missed Phillip as it plunged past him.

The ground shook. Flames exploded upwards, then went out. The battle was over.

No one moved or spoke.

Only Phillip's gasps for breath and the crackle of scattered fires broke the silence.

Dying embers and random sparks glowed red and gold, the only spot of colour in the bleak charred landscape. The last of the thorns shrivelled and disappeared like mist. A cool wind blew the dark clouds from the castle towers. Maleficent had been destroyed at last. But her curse on the Princess still remained.

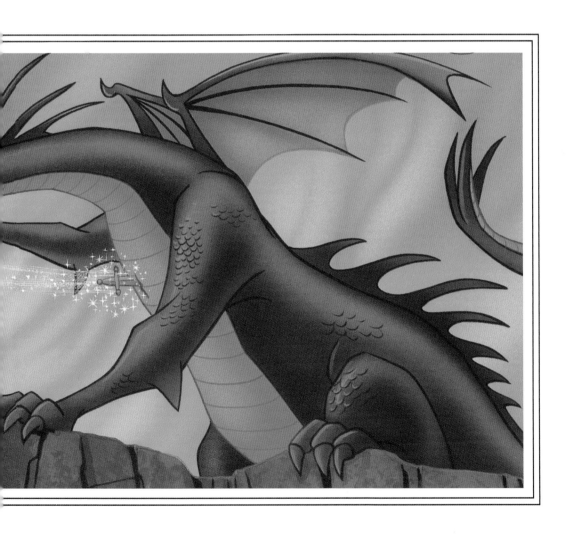

ome!" Flora beckoned Phillip.

Barely glancing at the people sleeping in the enchanted courtyard, he followed the fairies up the winding stairs to the tower where the Princess slept.

Phillip gazed at her. She was both peasant girl and princess, and he loved all of who she was with all his heart. He kissed her.

Aurora opened her eyes and looked at Phillip. "It's you," she said simply. He was the young man in the forest and a prince. And she loved all of who he was with all her heart.

The soldiers by the gates opened their eyes and picked up their swords and bows.

Knights and their horses, nobles and ladies in their fine clothes, lackeys and serving men, stable boys and laundresses awoke and continued their work and conversations as if nothing had happened. Dogs began to scratch, and the startled fleas awoke and dove for cover.

Banners and flags snapped and waved in the breeze as if embarrassed for having drooped, and now wanting to make up for the shame with extra energy. The fountain began to splash with a silvery chime.

In the throne room, King Stefan and the Queen awoke.

Stefan leaned over to King Hubert. "Forgive me, Hubert, you, ah, were saying?"

Hubert yawned. What was it he needed to tell Stefan? Then it came back to him.

"Well, to come right to the point, my son Phillip says he's going to –"

At that moment, trumpets rang out and a joyful murmur rose from the crowd.

All eyes turned to the grand stairway as Aurora and Phillip walked down it arm in arm.

"It's Aurora! She's here!" King Stefan cried.

"And Phillip!" Hubert added, with a relieved sigh. I will never understand that boy, he thought. But it didn't matter. Phillip was where he was supposed to be, and he was behaving like a proper prince. Finally.

King Stefan and the Queen gazed at their daughter as if they were seeing the first springtime.

She's so beautiful, the Queen thought.

She's home, King Stefan thought.

Aurora curtsied, suddenly shy and uncertain. Would they love her? Would she love them? But as they gathered her in their arms, her doubts disappeared. "My mother. My father." She said the words to herself. And she understood that they were part of who she was.

As the court musicians began to play, Phillip took Aurora in his arms and they began to waltz.

Merryweather watched
Aurora and Phillip dancing.

Something wasn't right. Merryweather pulled
out her wand and changed Aurora's gown to blue.
Much better, she thought.

But Flora was just as quick. "Pink!" she said,
waving her wand.

"Blue!" "Pink!" "Blue!" "Pink!" The colour battle
was on again.

Aurora never noticed.

Surrounded by magical clouds of blue and pink, she and her prince danced on ... just as they had "once upon a dream."

From the balcony, the fairies watched proudly. They had done their work well. But Fauna was sniffling.

"Why, Fauna, what's the matter, dear?" Flora asked.

"Oh, I just love happy endings," Fauna replied.

## THE END

True love conquers all.

*Briar Rose's*
*Forest Journal*

# Briar Rose is one year old today!

It seems like only yesterday that we came to the woodcutter's cottage with her as a tiny baby. I don't know where the time has gone!

Rose is growing so fast and changing so much every day, I want to keep a record of everything she does. I wish I had thought of it sooner. I bought this journal when it was my turn to go to the market, and we will take turns writing in it. Someday it will help us and her remember our time together in the forest. She's such a sweet, good child, and so curious and lively.

She likes to toddle around while I'm working in the garden.

She tries to catch the butterflies and "talks" to birds. They "talk" back to her, as if they understand each other perfectly.

The young forest animals are very curious about her. The other day, a baby bunny hopped up with a daisy in its mouth and dropped it at Rose's feet!

I think the animals know how sweet she is and that there's no harm in any of us.

First published in 2008 by Parragon

1 3 5 7 9 10 8 6 4 2

© Disney 2008

Printed and bound in China

ISBN 978-1-4075-2586-0

**M**any years
they had longed for
a *child*, and finally
their wish was granted...

First published in 2008 by Parragon

1 3 5 7 9 10 8 6 4 2

© Disney 2008

Printed and bound in China

ISBN 978-1-4075-2586-0

**M**any years
they had longed for
a *child*, and finally
their wish was granted...